It was autumn, and colourful leaves carpeted Bluebell Wood. Rabbit sat on top of Crow Hill looking down on the woodland. His nose twitched as he enjoyed the smells of the crisp morning and thought about the exciting day ahead.

Today it was Hare's Great Race. The Great Race had been held every year for many years. It was a chance for all the young hares to come along and show off their courage, speed and fitness as they raced around the woodland collecting mementos.

Rabbit's good friend Hare had started the race because of his great talent for running. This was the first year the race had been held without Hare. He had died a year ago and he was buried on top of Crow Hill. From where Rabbit sat he could see the young oaks that were now growing on the grave. Rabbit remembered how he had put acorns in Hare's coffin as a goodbye gift. The acorns reminded him of the memory box they had made together in the final months of Hare's life. The box had acorns carved on the lid and contained many precious items that had belonged to Hare including his smooth, white 'moon-gazing' stone, a string of conkers and a special friendship stick.

Rabbit was looking forward to the day ahead. He had learnt over the last year that after someone we love dies the memory of them can live on in our hearts. It's as if a tiny spark of their special flickering flame of life carries on glowing forever. Today he could feel Hare's tiny spark glowing even more brightly as he was remembered by all of Bluebell Wood.

By afternoon the hillside was transformed as the woodland animals gathered, chattering excitedly. Now the leaves had fallen it was easy to see the course of the race. Rabbit had found a good viewing point with his friend Buzzard.

As Rabbit sat waiting for the start, he felt so many different feelings. One minute he was sad that Hare was not chatting to the contestants on the starting line. The next his heart felt full of pride that he had been a special friend of Hare's.

Buzzard guessed how Rabbit was feeling and said, "Learning to live without someone you love takes a while. I think watching this race will feel a bit like how this last year has felt without Hare, full of ups and downs, challenges and triumphs. Today is not just about remembering Hare and celebrating life, but also realising how well you have done over the last year."

Buzzard and Rabbit watched as the young hares lined up to start racing. Old Badger was giving them a final talk about fairness and being sporting. Hare had been very strict about that sort of thing. It reminded Rabbit of a story Buzzard had told him when he had overheard Rabbit telling his friends how wonderful and perfect Hare had been.

Buzzard told them that Hare, when he was young, had been caught cheating and fighting during a race and then boasting about it afterwards. Buzzard said that just because someone has died doesn't mean that they were perfect when they were alive. "Hare had good and bad bits just like everyone else," he said.

Rabbit thought quietly for a moment. He had done a lot of fighting and arguing this past year. Buzzard and mum had explained to him that this was because he felt so cross that Hare had died. Some days he felt he might explode with angry feelings and he would just run and run as fast as he could to release all the feelings in his body.

Suddenly the starting branch went CRACK, making Rabbit jump. The race had begun, the young hares were off and running. The first part of the race was through thick undergrowth. As they ran through the dense woodland, the hares needed to be agile to squeeze through the narrow spaces. A couple of the hares were bouncing off the sides of trees and doing dangerous twists and turns in the air. This sort of acrobatics was new this year and Rabbit was impressed. He thought Hare would have loved it too.

Rabbit thought about the last year. He had often felt like he was upside down and inside out. One minute he was crying, missing Hare and wanting to be alone, and at other times he was enjoying life with his friends. Sometimes he had felt bad for enjoying himself when Hare was no longer here. Buzzard had told him very gently that laughing and having fun is part of being alive. Rabbit knew Hare would not have wanted him to feel sad all the time. Hare had believed in everyone enjoying themselves and shining their light as brightly as they could in the world.

All of a sudden a gasp went through the woodland; a young fox had run across the path of the runners, causing chaos. One of the hares fell over trying to avoid crashing into Fox Cub, while another fell against a tree stump. It reminded Rabbit of those sad moments that take you by surprise; he had found those the hardest to deal with.

One particular day this summer, he had been happily playing with his friends. As they were running through the wood they were calling out every time they saw a butterfly. This had made him remember how Hare had taught him the names of all the woodland butterflies. Suddenly he had felt very sad and really missed his friend and he didn't want to play any more.

On the race course, the hares had picked themselves up and were scrabbling around in the undergrowth looking for a sycamore key, the first memory item. As they each found one, they handed it over to a judge and ran on.

They had now reached the Badger Run. Most of the woodland thought this was the most difficult part of the race. The hares had to find their way through a maze of joined-together badger setts, and collect a conker. As hares don't live underground, going through the Badger Run was frightening. They had to use their whiskers and night-time eyes to find their way through, and every year one or more would get lost and need rescuing.

Rabbit wasn't scared of the dark at all. He loved his homely, dark burrow, but he could imagine how it might feel to a hare. Earlier in the year Buzzard had used the Badger Run as a way of helping Rabbit understand some difficult feelings.

Over the winter Rabbit had felt very unhappy. Life wasn't fun any more. He didn't feel like joining in with his friends or eating any of his favourite dandelion treats. All he wanted was to be with his family in their safe, warm burrow. He spent lots of time looking through the memory box that Hare had given him and remembering the stories that Hare had told him.

Buzzard had explained that after someone dies we can feel very, very sad. Our body may feel heavy and tired and we lose touch with our own "flickering flame of life" and the things that make us happy. This can feel like being in a long dark tunnel just like the Badger Run. Sometimes you feel lost and someone has to come and help you find yourself again. Rabbit felt glad to have had Buzzard and his family to help him.

The woodland was suddenly in uproar. Everyone was counting the hares out of the tunnel: one, two, three, four, five … where was number six? One hare was missing! The other hares handed over their conkers and ran on. The judges hung around the entrance, occasionally looking into the wide opening. Eventually Old Fox called into the hole, "Hellooooo." Minutes passed in silence; the whole woodland seemed to be holding its breath… waiting. Suddenly, in a rustle of twigs and leaves, a hare ran out of the tunnel, dropped a conker at the feet of a surprised Old Fox and ran on into the race. The whole woodland let out a sigh of relief and cheered him on.

The next bit was the stream crossing. This was Rabbit's favourite part of the race. As they watched the hares jump into the fast-moving stream, he thought how brave they were. "I don't think I'd like to jump into a stream, find a stone and then scramble out the other side," he said to Buzzard.

Buzzard laughed. "There are lots of ways to be brave, young Rabbit. I think you showed great courage last year after Hare died. It can be hard to do even everyday things when you are missing someone."

"Yes, it was hard," said Rabbit, "but it helped to talk to Hare in my head and ask what I should do. Even now when I need help, I still talk to Hare and I look at the 'moon-gazing' white stone in the memory box. It reminds me of Hare's great wisdom."

By now the hares were tired. They had all swum across the stream, found a smooth white stone and were on to the final leg of the race.

This was the sprint towards the finishing line and they just had to run as fast as they could. None of their legs looked bouncy anymore; each of them looked as if they were carrying a tree trunk across their shoulders.

Rabbit remembered how tired he used to feel in the first few months after Hare died. His body used to hurt in so many places, it was as if different parts of his body had to say goodbye to his dear friend. His heart and chest ached when he remembered their hugs and how Hare had loved him. His legs ached when he remembered walking and talking with Hare through the woodland. Sometimes even his ears had ached because he missed hearing all Hare's stories. For a time Rabbit had been worried he was ill. Dr. Owl had told him that aches and pains are normal and part of learning to go on living without someone we love very much.

Finally the woodland erupted in noisy celebration. What a triumph it was! All the hares were over the finishing line and being greeted by family and friends. The judges brought forward the mementos that the hares had collected during the race. These were presented to each contestant in a small conker box with an acorn on the lid. The winner was awarded a string of acorns, which was placed around their neck by Old Badger.

Afterwards, as Rabbit and all his friends enjoyed a celebration picnic, Rabbit thought what a special day it had been. Even though Hare wasn't there anymore, his memory lived on in the spirit of the race and was marked by the special conker boxes given to the contestants.

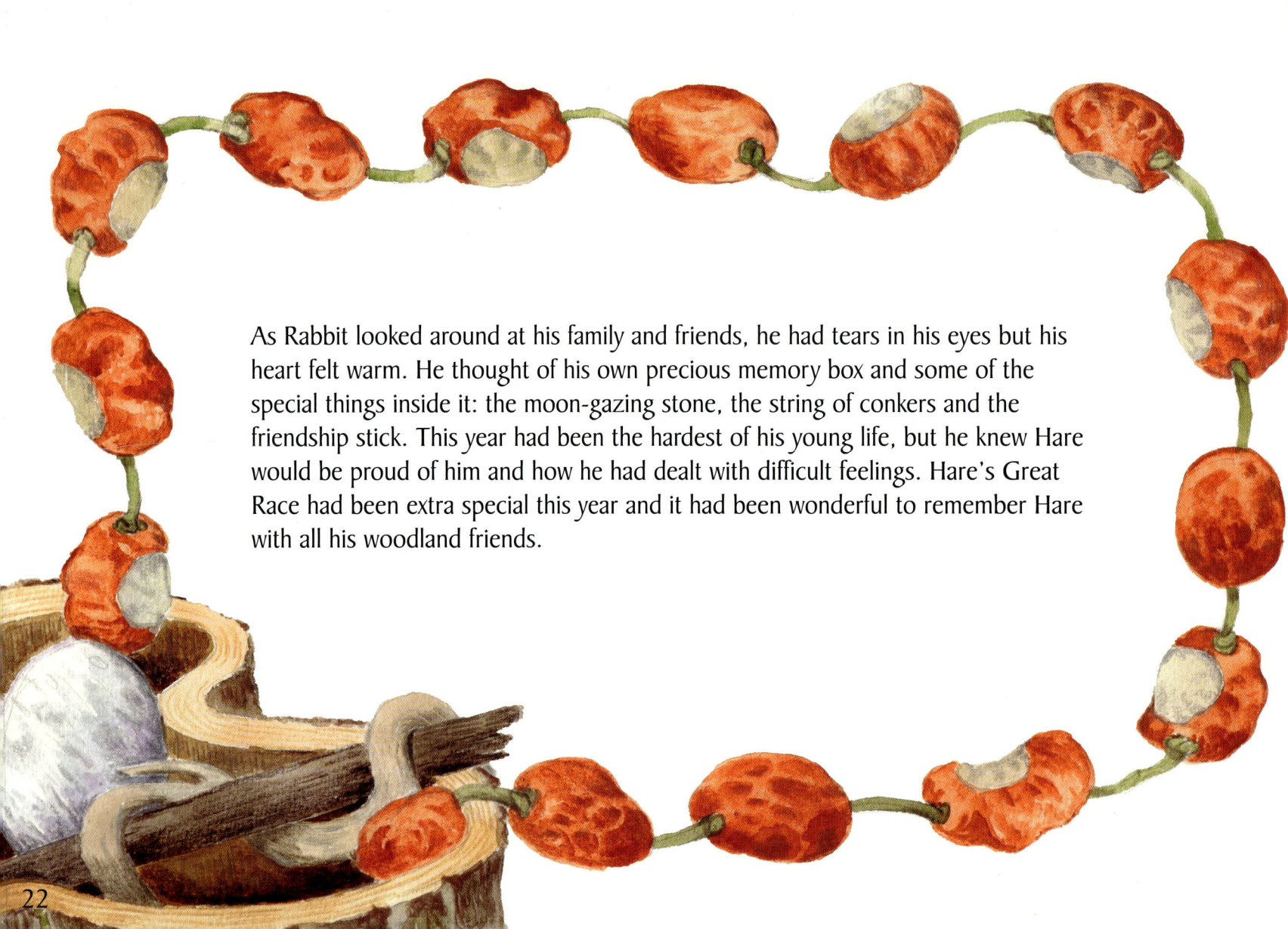

As Rabbit looked around at his family and friends, he had tears in his eyes but his heart felt warm. He thought of his own precious memory box and some of the special things inside it: the moon-gazing stone, the string of conkers and the friendship stick. This year had been the hardest of his young life, but he knew Hare would be proud of him and how he had dealt with difficult feelings. Hare's Great Race had been extra special this year and it had been wonderful to remember Hare with all his woodland friends.

Guidance notes for adults

Remembering Hare is aimed at 5-9 year olds who have experienced the death of someone they love. The story is intended to be shared and talked about between an adult and child. It can be helpful for children to simply re-read the story, repeatedly, like other stories. Once you both have a sense of familiarity with its contents, it can be used as and when questions arise.

Children in this age bracket will have great variations in how they understand death. Younger children will be very curious and, if they feel they are allowed, will ask lots of questions. They are likely to repeat the same questions at different developmental stages which can sometimes feel frustrating for their carers. However, this does not mean that you have failed to answer their questions, but simply that they now have a deeper understanding and so require more information. They will generally not be able to put into words how they feel and will look to close adults to help them understand their feelings.

Younger children in this age range generally have great imaginations, also known as 'magical thinking'. Mostly they do not understand the finality of death and may be expecting to see the person again, or they may believe that they were responsible for the person's death in some way.

Older children in this age range may well understand the finality of death but may actively begin to hide their feelings, not wanting to appear babyish, or risk upsetting others. Their new understanding of death, and therefore their own mortality and of those they love, may generate a huge amount of anxiety and fear.

Remembering Hare touches on a number of themes that will help you be supportive to a child who is grieving.

1. Support ~ *Buzzard is a wise and supportive friend*

Children can feel isolated and alone when someone close to them has died. All children will respond differently to bereavement and need different support depending on their age, personality, history of previous losses and the relationship they had with the person who died. However, all children will need: honest age-appropriate answers to their questions; time and space to ask the questions they need; help to make sense of physical and emotional feelings; help to hold on to memories; to know that what they are feeling is normal; physical comforting and affection.

2. Sharing memories ~ *Rabbit and Buzzard share their memories of Hare together. Buzzard affirms Rabbit's memories and puts them into perspective so he can appreciate the legacy of Hare's life.*

For children who have experienced the death of someone significant to them, celebrating memories is an essential part of learning to live without that person. Telling and retelling stories of time spent together help embed in their minds experiences that help define their childhood.

Children may feel uncomfortable sharing their own memories for fear of upsetting others, so sharing your own memories of that person will give them permission to do the same.

In the early part of grieving, sharing memories brings up sad feelings so children may need reassuring that feeling sad is a natural part of learning to live without someone. Children will interpret memories differently depending on their age and stage of development. Up until the age of about 8, they often slip into a fantasy world, embellishing stories and memories. By about age 9, most children are more in touch with the real world.

3. Memory boxes ~ *Rabbit returns time and time again to the comforting stories and mementoes in Hare's memory box*

Whatever a child's age, memory boxes, or treasure chests, are a way of consciously sharing and 'banking' memories of a person after their death.

Most memories are visual - pictures we hold in our head, which can be stimulated and refreshed by outside triggers and these triggers come from all of our senses. The senses of touch and smell for children can be particularly evocative. The close interaction of touching, cuddling and soothing which forms part of the early bonding in a relationship, and which releases 'feel good' chemicals in the body, can be re-awakened by the feel of 'dad's old jumper', or the smell of 'mum's perfume'. So, when putting a memory box together with a child, it may be worth thinking how you can stimulate all their senses.

4. Emotional ups and downs ~ *Buzzard helps Rabbit make sense of topsy-turvy feelings*

Grief is made up of many different feelings including fear, anger and sadness. Children tend to dip in and out of grief; they are naturally optimistic and full of life and so do not dwell on unhappy feelings. This can sometimes be disconcerting for the adults around them, who are feeling overwhelmed with a mixture of feelings about death, and questioning how best to support their child. Children may also hide their feelings or swallow back tears for fear of upsetting others. It is important that children are encouraged to express how they feel and they learn how to do this by watching the adults around them. Therefore showing your feelings and sharing with children how you feel will encourage them to do the same.

5. Sadness ~ *Buzzard explained that grief can feel like being lost in a long, dark badger run, or 'up and down' just like the hares in the race, or like falling over something unexpected.*

The sadness of grief can be felt in many different ways. It can feel heavy, deep and prolonged, like a general malaise that dampens our whole experience of life, affecting how we sleep, eat and interact with others. It can also be experienced as intensely painful moments as we stumble across reminders in our day-to-day life that someone special has died.

6. Anger ~ *Rabbit argued and fought after Hare had died; he was so cross that Hare had left him*

Feeling angry is a normal response to loss and bereavement. Younger children often don't have the understanding and words to express their feelings. Therefore sadness is often expressed as angry outbursts, tantrums, and aggression towards themselves or others.

Children may harbour feelings of it being their fault in some way, 'if only I'd been nicer', 'done as I was told', 'tidied my room' maybe it wouldn't have happened. When a child says, 'it's not fair', all we can do is agree and say that often life isn't fair but reassure them that the death is nothing to do with anything they did or didn't do.

If a child feels angry it can help to find healthy ways to express this. These could be: punching a pillow or cushion; scribbling or drawing in a particular 'angry' colour or in an 'angry' book; physical activity, such as running, bouncing on a trampoline or kicking a ball.

7. Physical feelings ~ *Dr Owl reassured Rabbit about his aching body*

It is completely normal to have a physical response to grief. Here are a few of the common ones: tummy upsets and pains; aching/weak muscles; tight chest; tight or sore throat; headaches; tension throughout the whole body.

Research has shown that a chemical change occurs within the body as a result of loss and bereavement. When we form a close attachment to someone the mutual love and affection releases 'feel good' chemicals. When this attachment is broken we experience the 'withdrawal' of these chemicals which affects our whole being. Physical closeness and comfort is therefore essential to ease the pain of grief. Explaining the connections for children about bodily sensations will take away any anxiety about aches and pains they may have.

> **To download some free family activities which you might also find useful, please go to www.sayinggoodbyematters.com**